Paula Scollan is a practising solicitor and she owns general practices in Leitrim and Dublin. Paula is also a legal affairs columnist with the Leitrim Observer newspaper. Her interests include human rights, travel, photography, art, film and music. She has provided a long standing and committed volunteer service with various free legal advice centres. In her previous life Paula worked in community pharmacies, methadone clinics and St Luke's oncology hospital. She studied psychology, television direction and production, worked in legal clinics in New York, worked as a criminal defence lawyer in Tallaght, worked as a current affairs monitor, taught English and dancing to nuns from the Congo, taught in the international study centre, researched the implications of health legislation in Ireland, explored the world at every possible opportunity, wrote and painted along the way.

To Setanta, Solomon and Senan who continue to make it worthwhile, and to Padraig, thanks and ever thanks.

PAULA SCOLLAN

SOTTO VOCE

AUSTIN MACAULEY
PUBLISHERS LTD.

A CIP catalogue record for this title is available from the British Library.

ISBN 9781786290830 (Paperback)
ISBN 9781786290847 (Hardback)
ISBN 9781786290854 (E-Book)

www.austinmacauley.com

First Published (2016)
Austin Macauley Publishers Ltd.
25 Canada Square
Canary Wharf
London
E14 5LQ

Acknowledgments

I wish to thank Tom Haynes for his generosity and skill as a publisher and editor.

I am also very grateful to friends and family for their unstinting support and enthusiasm. My thanks to Donal O'Grady and Claire McGovern at the Observer for the opportunity they extended to me. And my heartfelt gratitude to Padraig, Setanta, Solomon and Senan for their constant encouragement and above all humour.

All proceeds from the sale of this book will go to the Innocence Project. The Innocence Project is an international organisation dedicated to exonerating wrongfully convicted individuals and reforming the criminal justice system to prevent future injustice. The project provides pro bono legal and investigative services to people trying to prove their innocence. DNA and other evidence is re-examined where there are claims of wrongful conviction. Since it began in 1992, hundreds of people have been exonerated in the USA. Many of those had served time on death row and were convicted because of eyewitness misidentification, jailhouse snitches, sloppy police work, corrupt prosecutors, incompetent or overburdened defence attorneys or improper forensic science and informants, that is, statements from people with incentives to testify.

One out of four wrongfully convicted made a false confession or incriminating statement. Exhaustion from an overnight search, long interrogation, mental illness or psychological vulnerability, drugs, alcohol, fear of violence, fear of the death penalty, the threat of a harsh sentence, misunderstanding the situation and coercion are just some of the reasons leading to a false confession.

The Innocence Project has expanded to most American states. Projects inspired by the success of the American model have been transposed to countries worldwide. The Irish Innocence Project was founded in 2009 and is currently reviewing 20 active post conviction cases.

The author has worked with the Innocence Project in the past and she has always maintained a keen interest in the cases. These are real lives, real cases, often shocking and very moving. It's about having a sense of justice. Those working with the Innocence Project want to do their best for the clients they represent. One innocent in jail is one too many.

In purchasing this book, you are contributing to the service of a fair justice system for all and the author thanks you sincerely for that. Let us show dignity, compassion and respect for all.

Contents

Je l'aime

Sitting, loving
Laughter interrupting
Our open ears
Chasing us closer
To every hour
Here together and
There for now and
Then forever
While tilting glances
Fade, awakening our
Compiled completion
Interesting freedom
Elsewhere still free
Strumming outside madness
Connecting out sometimes
Forgotten highs.

Indifference

As I sit here overlooking time
The city drifts with indifference
Thwarted aims, beaten minds
Inducing unrealised damnation
And as I seek its apprehension
There is only pain

Until aged twelve
I wandered the woven streets
Admired the moon
Until it closed behind me
Watched the people rushing past
With grace against the wind

Going about their business
Tending to their flocks
Eyes blind to my beginnings
Silent strategy to the estranged.
Better than pity or scorn
It is regretful that we never found

A way to bridge the gap
Earth has moved and
Winter drips
My heart has missed a beat
I beat at the bars
And God opened the door

I no longer live in a box
By the steps of city hall
And as forensics seek
Its comprehension
There is only pain

Drifting Away

Live for now
Live for peace
Open up your mind
Remain all at one
Try, cool, and stay someone
Who really cares

Living looking no despair
Loving complete through time
Loan out your mind
Selves complete
Play completes
Peace at once

Surrender break your mould
Offer gold
Care while there
Penny fools, broken rules
Laughing looking
Blinding dreams.

Mountjoy Women's Prison

I see her long hair now
Tangled, uneasy
Her arms scratched
Her white face
Opposite mine in
Mountjoy Women's
Prison

I spoke of arraignment
Guilty she said
What does it matter
A rest in The Joy
Away from the filthy

I move into the day
Sitting in the courts
Listen to stories
Brought to justice
As life gallops past.
Just another girl
Her dreams stolen by
The magpie commodore

And I felt I knew her
Unfinished karma
From a life past
I watched as the guard took
Her away to
Drink methadone in her tea

Until she is ready again,
Newly clad and fragrant, to
Sell her body to walk the
Streets to feed her habit.
Sun will come and frost and
I see her walking into the
Slow twilight of her life.

Zephyr Blows

Zephyr wanders over Mumbai
Sweeping ghostly
Slowly to Paris
An ever present shadow lurking
In the minds
Of frightened faces
Like a self-conceited uninvited serpent
He gallops far beyond the borders
On the ground to Baghdad

Guiding time and warping thoughts
Surviving in a sea of shadows
A million thoughts are flung by the Beirut gale
While a baron land of burnt out brands
Ebb softly in the Kenyan darkness
Weeping for the flame
Idolatry of anger over Yemen
Somalia, Libya, Iraq and Sudan
The mendicant drifts on

Fatima Gate

At Fatima Gate you say
At the gate she died
Died you say
Died in labour
In labour
Unable to cross the border
The border to her house
Lying dead in the afterbirth
Dead in the afterbirth
A Palestinian woman
Dead Palestinian mother
Because of men drawing
Lines in the sand
Men drawing lines in the sand.

Ghostly she had walked in tears
Through the wind gritted dust
From her past lover's home
To the border
Carrying her unborn child
Conceived in hurried love.
Weeks before she celebrated
Her birthday
Bewildered and twenty-two.
She spoke three languages
Liked bright clothes and music.

They buried them quickly
Never mentioned them again
Two young bodies laid to rest
In the dark soil
Only birds disturb the quiet now.

Clifden

In a barren of wilderness
We stopped and stared
At a silent wind
And silver rocks

A haunting landscape
Left its mark
And pierced the hearts
Of those gone before

A million thoughts
Are stored in this land
And the ponies
Stare close by

A peaceful world
By the mottled lake
The moonlight sonata
Its intricate delight

A cluster of trees
In furtive hiding
A virginal deliverance
Not letting go

Feel your heart at peace
After riding the storm
Sitting under the rain
In Clifden

Butterflies

Ahmad
Mohammed
Ali
Walking O'Connell Street
A white Christmas day.
Three souvenirs
From Beirut
Under the lights their
First day in Dublin
Seeking protection political
Asylum.

Dancing butterflies
Wild in their tummies
Drifting on in silence
Experiencing
Something new.

Ali was a spy
Coby said
Coby is Jewish
He has a view.
Mohammed the shi'i
Liked flipping burgers.
Ahmed was the fun one
'Took a walk on the
Wild side' did not
Carry a gun.

Fighting at fourteen
Education was for the
Privileged ones.
But Dublin English is
Difficult to forget

Soon Ahmed had the
'All right love'
He blended, mingled
Found new love.
Mohammed got a girlfriend
Ali died on a cold
Wednesday night in
Saint Luke's Oncology unit.
May Allah bless them
Now.

Perdition

The world was howling with a wind of anger
Perforating a blanket of bedraggled blue
Sitting at the door of a Turkish church
Was a worn faced Syrian and a child of
Paralyzed youth to her breast

With a ruffled arm
She held out a stained hand
Pitifully crying for kindness
Indifferent to their judgement on her
Their cowardice

Requiem echoed within the walls and
One added a shade of mercy
But those who had gone before
Coalesced to their homes
A cold goodnight

I left her
A beacon of hopelessness
Is this all we can do
Beyond the borders
For the damned?

Court 44

Bridewell
Court 44
I bleedin
Love ya
Ma

Thanks for that Ma
Tell Da I love him
Bleedin pigs
Thanks Ma
Love ya Ma

All right love
See ya sweetheart
Up in clover
Was at the
Bleedin dentist judge

Wasn't me
I swear ya right
It wasn't me
Collect the baby
Will ya love?

I'll wait for ya Johnny
I'll be here
Love ya pet
See ya Tuesday
Alright love

In The Day

Living in the day
Placing time on hold
Making life a ball
Days cool not sold
Packing in old dreams
Looking on in smiles
Hopelessly in love
Over spilling time
Interest comes again
Happy in a wheel
Rolling out the pure
Sending up the rules
Laughter closes in
Even round our bend
Drawing near to sight
Pass around that smile again

One Track Celtic Tiger

Dromad tickets please
Checking all tickets for Dromad
Want to be Dali fingers oils
Vacant mind is silent in intricate dream
Ivy league funkster consumes the darkness
Black shuck black shuck
Bows his pierced eyebrow
Frightened to talk to the granny next to him
I, lost in thought travelling backwards
Want to dance among the bluebells in the valley
Just before we cross the lake
Communication on the Sligo-Dublin train

We stop in Mullingar
Grey eyes looked dirty, retro
Sit here
Take my mind's space
On to Enfield
Best to buy some expensive cheap Merlot
Cheese and onion to caress the journey
Forestry hides the ominous gaps
Where cattle score
We stop to a halt
One track Celtic tiger
We await the Dublin train

She drops her oils
Produces a laptop
We cross the river
What beautiful new ditches
And shiny yellow diggers
And people on a hill where the dead sleep

Mullingar tickets please
Checking all tickets for Mullingar and Enfield
Mini marches up the
Network catering with biscuits
Down town Maigh Nuad
Students of Hamlet, Theology
And philosophical night life evacuate.
On past Leixlip, brick by brick of it
In undulating boredom
Clonsilla's sense of community
Last of 'Produit de France'

Under the bridge
Past the graffiti crumbling pavements
Drumcondra's back gardens
The concrete walls of the flats
Welcome to Dublin Connolly
The selfless culture of
Overcrowded hospitality
And irregular streets
Up Amien street
An electrified city
On home to Ranelagh.

Midnight Calling

Midnight call to
Tallaght Garda station
A bloody nose
Shaking hands
Who beat you son?

A cigarette?
Yes,
What happened, Wayne?
The alarm buzzed as I left
I just wanted a ring
For my girlfriend.
Who beat you?
I do not know.

Wayne was twenty two
The father of one
Little boy in Jobstown
With big blue eyes
And sallow skin
Impossible to win
Who wants to be a
Bug when he grows
Up so he can
Walk on the roof.

I gave him a
Sandwich
We talked a while
I promised to come
Back and sort it.

Lefkosia

Old city
In a Venetian wall
Where once the Ottomans
And British ruled.

Where Famagusta gate
Giulio's tunnel of glory
And Pafos is poised
Between Greek and Turkish purity.

Holy Cross in dead zone
Its Turkish rear
In a land of apartheid
And the victims of Deryneia
Will you cross the green line
In Europe's last divided city?
Will you smile in the weary eye
Of the United Nations
In no man's land?

A Shapely Orb

Sitting
Rotting
In Mountjoy Prison
I am reminded of
The sponge I thought
Was a rock.

I hit him on the head
He did not fall
The old man in
Dartmouth square.
He called his son
Who called the guards

An intruder in the house.
They arrested me
I did not care
I was high as a beam
Walking on air

Now as I sit here
Doing my time
I think of that
Sponge
And what might
Have been mine.

Temperance

Love, Life
Lonely man
Loving Sylvia
Lovely child
River run
Poodle wild
Pure and timeless
A dreamed up world
Anonymous happy feeling
Eternal
Alternative
Freedom to the great
Sea of being from
Which we all come
And to which
We will return.

Baby Poula

Born in Holles Street
Cloudy night of my
Twenty first
Birthday
Little girl refugee
I sheltered you.
From war torn Beirut
To a flat in Rathmines
Two worlds meet.
Named in my honour
In a cradle by the
Door, your mummy
Hanna plaited my
Hair, told me of
Secret passions
Brutal bombs
Shattered dreams.
Brothers fought
Your uncle died
Hiding in a bombed
Out house in Barbour.
Escaping to London
Dublin
Pregnant in the night.
You are here now
Safe in this city
And I will see that
You are alright.
The cloud moved
You made your own
Way like a robin
I miss you.
And I know that
You will raise the

Lebanese flag
One day
Safe in your own
Home town.

Beirut Love

I was working as
A waitress in the
Wexford Inn
When I met you
Sitting with your
Irish friend Jimmy
Who drank gin and
You drank water.
You made a bet that I
Would date you.
I said no, again and
Again, no until I
Gave in.

You loved me and
We shared much fun
From Dublin to London
At weekends to meet
Our brothers all
Eleven of them on
Political asylum in
A hotel in Westminster.

New Year's Eve
At Big Ben
And I on your
Brother's shoulders
Not to be trampled
By people and pigeons
Fast women in uniform
On slow horses.

Our trips to
Cyprus to cross
The border to
Beirut at nightfall
Hiding in bombed
Out houses
To visit our sisters
In Barbour who
Cherished us.

Beautiful city
In pain broken by
Turmoil once
Paris of the
Middle East
Home of Fairuz
A gem and
Bankers' paradise

It was Nineteen
Ninety Two
And I was seventeen.
We were brave
You and I
Not afraid of the war
Not afraid of destruction.

I was twenty two when
I left you on a
Cold Dublin night.
I sometimes think of
You and her now.

Child of Cairo

Splendour of Cleopatra's
Empire shimmering in
The desert
Mystery of the Sphinx and
Jewel of the Nile.
Domain of the Pharaohs
Tut-Ankh-Amon
Here on the
Giza plateau
Heart of
Civilisation and
Magnificent wonder
Child of Cairo
Begging
For one Cypriot pound.

Cloverhill Detention Centre

Out they gallop
The boys in
Cloverhill
Monkeys I'm advised
As they descend.
Ward you're mine
I shout as he
Gives me a grin.
Prison officer nods
It's him again.
Glad they sent you
Ward says
I didn't like the
Other one.
How you pleading?
Not guilty
My job done.
Get the bus
Back to Tallaght.
Wait Ward said
Get my car keys in
Reception
Give them to Sharon
She needs to drive
Our baby.
Ward I said
Handling stolen goods
Not this one.

I Had a Dream

Pot of Mongolian
Mutton stew
Talk from the heart with
Loving respect in Vietnam.
From Dubai to Brighton
Work fight and die for it
Right of the
Child everywhere.
Equality, a home
Heartbreak and it is
Alright to cry
Beautiful life.
The real Miss Saigon here
Shine in every way
Growing better and better.

Industrial school system
Poverty, betrayal on a
Single real journey of
Existence
A good kind of crazy.
Mama Tina of
The Phoenix Park
Gluing the pieces of a
World like wet sand
Protection of the shore.
Brilliant sunshine
Radiant warm.
You had a dream
And you won.
'...Ring a ring a rosy
As the lights decline
I remember Dublin city in
The rare ould times...'

Kalabraki

Florid recollections
Memory lapse in
Mysterious tales
Independent facts

Flooded minds
Mind games in
Complicated sequences
Tailored facts

Memories improve
Hospitality box
Radars of deception
Administrative facts

Renewed anticipation
New can of worms, alas
A new day is dawning
Of festive facts

Mohammedan Mother

Educated in London
He liked English girls
Football and cake
What freedoms might be had

Shopping in Harrods
Feeding the pigeons in
Trafalgar Square
Loving Dickinson
Austin, Astaire
All consuming Brontë

Watching the changing of
The guard at
Buckingham palace
Catching a movie at
Notting Hill

Until he got the call
Training for his motherland
The noble Quran firmly
Planted in his head
Be strong, you are in
Allah's hands

'I testify that there is
No God but Allah
Hasten to prayer
Hasten to welfare
Hasten to the best of acts
There is no God but
Allah and I am a
Successful Muslim'

He straps the bomb
To his chest
He walks towards the light
He looked and saw
His future
Something huge had awoken

Victory over fear he
Pressed on
With a still throat and
Deep dark eyes
Feet planted firmly on
The ground
After a moment
He was gone.

In a black starless night
A Mohammedan mother
Is hiding her face
In a yashmak guise
Her babies dying
Innocent victims
Of just another bomb

Who will wipe the
Cluster of tears from
The eyes of the
Mother of Iraq?

With You

Cuvee Montplo
Grenache Merlot
Dearest Julien
Pringles, caramel
Gourmet lust entwine
Chose life sun
Rugby socks
Playtex bras
Never die of wanting
Light a cigarette
And lose yourself
Mirrored reflections
Within our souls
You and I together
Freedom at last

Ostend

We never came here together, you and I
And perhaps that is why
All the things I've wished to say
Are made much easier this way

I did not notice so clearly then, as I do now
All the love and kindness is due
To you and to you alone
For all the beautiful qualities that you have shown

To have given so little, yet received so much
May forever stain my heart
Yet from these deepest, dearest, thoughts and feelings
I shall never be apart.

Persona Grata

Why
He sprays
Klein, dines
Lies to
Save his pride
The best in
An insecure guise
Works in the cafe where
He cleans and
Sells himself
When midnight passes.

Why
The men gathered
Like weeds
Hunters in the night
Stole his youth
Scorned him
Against the wire fence.
Courageously
He will rise again
Like the lapwing
Full of hope.

For he
Must eat
And breathe
And smell
Must live
And tell
Walk
And talk
And climb
The tree
Of his own life.

Push Ahead

Like to try some
Light the pot
Oven off, we're
Not that hot
Steal away
Save some skins
Just in case
The pusher rings
Give it all
Lay around
Be exactly where you're at

Change the story
In your head
Looking to the garden
Apple, plum and
Pear trees close by
In this space where
Your life is sat.

Looking forward your
Heart is opening
Infinite possibilities
Intimate times
Probing, engaging
Looking for purpose
Emotional reassurance
Physical sensation.
Quiet the intellect
Slow our lives to
Accept it.

Summer Of '92

Good and plucky boys
Cleaned Sarajevo
Straight as a die with
Artillery and snipers

Massacres
Expulsions and
Mass murder of
Innocence to

Kill our sons
Execute our fathers
Rape our daughters and
Eliminate all hope

Herd
Human mash
While the world
Is sleeping

September 11th

Pitiful darkness falls.
Sitting on the flowers
In a field of
Intimate distractions and
A cold wind of anger
While the warmth
From my tea
Trickles gently
Masking the mendicant

A beacon of tears
Under the moonlight
My mind engulfed
In this mellow taste
And the pigeons
Grow old in the meadows
A fox stares close by.
The wind calls and
I wrap my shawl tighter

Shadows lurk in
The blackness
But all I see are
The eyes in the sky
And they cannot tell me why
Three thousand souls
Are at peace
Gone to ground
In graveyards of all kinds

Buried in weather
Moss and ivy
Comrade, brother
Husband, lover
Sons and daughters
Mothers of life
And kindness
All fading
With the years.

The Phoenix

Bubbles of blood dripped
From a young mouth
Her body laid bare by
A pathologist
Sixteen years old
A school girl who
Liked pink hair and trainers
What pain could she have caused you?

Knee capped strangers
Boys too young to comprehend
Young men who liked
Fast cars and girls
What pain could they have caused you?

Terrorists guile
Sectarian sects
Who next?
A father's head on the pavement
Below a closed door
Seagulls cry
What pain could he have caused you?

A teenage boy off school
Sees something
He should not see
Pharisees petulant
Bullets rage
While Belfast sleeps
What pain could he have caused you?

Assailant
Soldiers' chore
Ship of fools no more
Maternal screams
Damien, darling David
Let the white chalked circle end

Vietnamese Boat Mother

A flimsy boat in the
South China Sea to
Malaysia and Tralee to
Dublin for
Freedom

With child and daughter
You fled Vietnam
Never to see your
Soldier, your true
Love again

Social isolation
Suffering few understand
Like a famine
Coffin ship to a
Strange land

Your baby son
Born in Ireland
Blind and deaf
A reminder of the
Harrowing sea

For thirty six years
You thought of your
One love, not knowing
Never knowing if
He made it

He will never meet
His son.
Your daughter in Maynooth
Teaching Anthropology
Proud mum

Nobel and strong
Vietnamese boat mother
Will carry on
Unsettled into life
Her mission drifting on.

Zante

Your magic charmed me
Little flower of the east
Not I alone but the Achaeans
Athenians and Spartans

You captivated the
Macedonians and with the
Fall of Constantinople came
Orsinis and Venetians to your rocky coast

French republicans, aristocrats
The British and the Turks
All wanted you
Radiant sun drenched isle

1953 could not kill your olive glow
Citrus smell or the pale eyes of your sea that
Penetrate your sandy shores and
Dream-like coves

Cantada called me
Like Solomos and Andreas
To drink the cool of your sea
Zante

Palmerston Park

Little boy hugs a tree
Talks to himself
Father walks the dog
Alongside his laughing heirs
Pele kicks a ball
Into a toddler's face
The sun shines
Behind a veil of white
Its radiance shines through
And I smile.

Empty beer cans, wine bottles
Tangle the grasses
Blackbird's song
Imposes on the conquered land
Edge of wilderness
Where the thorns of the roses
Catch at my dress
Out of mist and old trees
The red geraniums dance
In comfort and serenity.

Lilac, yew and daffodils that
Survived Spring
All laid by time and skill.
Reflecting passing clouds
Sun kissed buttercups and
Dandelions dancing alongside
Whispering weeping willows
Multipurpose compost
To nourish
And seed

Just then as an apparition
A flirtatious drizzle
A brush of a gentle wind
Caresses my ears
The white veil opens
Another Sunday
Afternoon alive
Inspired
Blessed and free
In Palmerston Park.

Back of a Bike

Looking good on the
Back of a bike
Leather clad in
Douglas

Girls from
West Shannon
Complete
Warrington men

Blazing the trail
Many have before done.
Scoping the island in a
Red Kawasaki

Tanned happy
White rum traders
Hovering angels
Katie and Ken

All night parties in
Ramsey
Sleeping on the floor
Of an Indian keeper's Inn.

Races over
TT fans moving on
A haunting silence
Sweeps the island

Until next year
Katie
Ken
Rev over again.

Belgrave Park

Mother breastfeeds her child
Munches on her crisps
Child cries
With potent euphony

Brown, white, red boys play ball
Precocious curly soldier
Sits in contemplation
Well done Emmanuel

Tan toned surrealist
Sits in surveillance
Arms outstretched
Susceptible to perfection

Mother kisses her baby
Sun shines
Smiles
Black hair glistens

Is a mother's devotion eternal?
Will I ever get a job?
I confidently hate
To work

Chinese, Spanish wanderlust
Wallowing in universal fun
So nice, so one
Powwow in our park

Queue in Victoria Street
Sign on, why bother when
The sun shines bright?
Earth, esquire is rich

Mother feeds child again
She nods
Beautiful green eyes
Straight white teeth

Bicycle chases a lorry past
Belgrave public spirit
Hey Emmanuel
Come here

You were fighting
No I was not
I was inspiring him
Can I have a drink?

Erudite from
Rathmines library, his
Cravat rallies
In our park

Cartwheels
Bald toddler, big
Belly in a belly top
Mobile patrol

More feeding
Legs espouse the sun in
Extravagant progress, rapt in
Probity

Couple plays frisbee
As freckles leave their mark
Glad I waxed my legs today
A tourist comes my way

Midday
Slattery's on the way
Pint my love, it's
Time to read my zen

Like Chaplin's autobiography
Wonderful book of
Urgent importance
Over to the swings

Four year old says
Kiss my ass
Blast, toddler's back again
Universal baby talk

White balls
Floating on high
Sprinkle the green
A connecting art

Bottom of the ocean one
Finds peace, on the road
On a mountainside
And Belgrave Park

Sun-kissed couple
Entrench the bench
Wrinkled arms
Entwined

Dandelions ransack
Their conquered city
And hold to ransom
Sweet Belgrave Park

Hide and seek
Chase instead
Arm in sling
Tyre swing

Elegant natives, squires
Erotic entourage of
Trusted eucalyptus
Eurasians flutter in

The golden chain of
The laburnum, rose
Daisies summer home
Belgrave Park.

Obituaries

Ecstasy in the Fiddler
Drummer Sammy
Downers in the night
Cathy save him
Lines taken in
Not read
Off his head

What a waste of
One so wise
Gentle, eloquent
Persuasively named
In the obituaries of
His own life.

Elphin Oak

Tall
Strong and proud
Overlooking time
Guardian of the meadows
Cattle and horses
Sycamore, beech
And dale
Shrouded in secrets
You know it all

Shelter of hawthorn
Buttercups and
Sparrows' nest
Home where the bees
Make their honey
And we laid
Setanta's canary in a
Cheese box to rest.

The hares at our feet
Alive and
Tame as they dance
Silent acclaim under a
Pale white-blue sky.

Did you see the big storm?
Did you see the bull fight?
Senan hiding in the
Icehouse and
Little Solomon
Riding ponies bare back
At night.

Who put you there?
The earth and the
Groundsman
From another life.

The sun shines strong
On you today
On the pigeons and
Spiders that fly
Crawl your way
Mother birds bringing
Food to their young.
It shines on the peace
Of this place
All that is past and
Yet to come.

Leaves changing from
Green to brown
What have you
Witnessed
Raised and fallen?
The day they built
Burned
Bishops Palace
Closed the grammar
School down

Did you admire Percy French,
Oliver Goldsmith?
Practice the Meta secret
Participating in this grand
Miracle called life.

Long to
Live in Smith Hill
Clooney Quinn or
Liss Adorn?
Spread your seeds in the
Deanery, Clouahee or
Mantua House.

What other abundance
Touched you in
The hundred or so years
That you have been?

Noble
Eloquent and proud
You will stand long
Celebrating life
After we
And our gold fish
Are all
Gone.

The Mines

Forty years I worked and toiled
In a black hole beneath the ground
From dawn till dusk
The black soot fell
In a soulless pit of despair

An economic holocaust
That's all there was
For the patriotic
Who stayed for love of a
Bottomless pit of
Western soil

The self-inflicted hardship
Of a father's love
The Arigna Mines
Cursed us, saved us
Enslaved us
Savaged us
Sustained us and
Sold us
All my children
Love me.

Enjoy the Colours

Let's drink the bottle neat
Get lushed under Rathmines rain
Let's dance till dawn
To Nina Simone
Let's buy a Rasher painting
Hang it with affection
Let's feed the mice
And munch nachos in Bruges
Let's drive
From New York to San Francisco
Let's pretend you're Ned Kelly
Passionate Robin Hood
Let's never get expensive
Be forever twenty-two
Kiss in Venice.
Let's make love in Paris
The kind of love you
Surrender to it and it
Surrenders to you
Let's call that fisherman in Kerry
Sink radioactive vodka
Gate-crash orderly emotions
Let's dive in Malta
Soak in healing waters
Swim with dolphins
Let's enjoy the colours on
The palette that is our life
Let's go to Mexico
Before life calls time.

Eternal India

Monsoon girl
In a pretty yellow sari
Celebrating the festival
Of light in my house
With a warm open smile
And a friendly heart

You introduced me to
Twenty seven masterpieces
Of classical glory
Triumphs of liberation
Recriminations of partition

From the flood to the bomb
An epic of monuments
Temples and tombs
Mughal conquests
The glory of Islam
And British rule

Himalayas
An abode of Gods
Ganges and Brahmaputra
Enmesh our
Most extensive delta

Formidable dynasties
Where teachings of Buddha
Create a galaxy of integrity
An eloquent testimony
That is sculptural India

71

On a Broken Wave

"Light up my darkness,"
Said the squirrel to the crow
"I'm out of fuel this morning."
"Why not ask the raven
He seems pretty hip,"
Said a drunken serpent
Sipping on a drunken
Seagull's cider
Cheering up a silent
Playful swallow snorting
A squirrel's burnt out clay tree
Once a haven.

Surrender to Love

Together and forever
Together as two
Nowhere in between
Still and pure
Content tonight
Making love hours nigh
Opening our minds
Freedom beckons hearts
Longing summer fun
Please take my space
Look into these eyes
Wakening a star
Seasons harmonise
Early morning mist
Trickle down my heart
Contemplating time
Muse here today.

Dreamer

Sometimes I swallow
Weeks on end
Definitely tomorrow
Well sometime this year
Thinking back in silence
Heckles fill the air
Hoping full of certainty
Infantile despair

Let's sit around a table
You can bring the chairs
Open all our hatred
And relax with a beer

Winding up the meeting
Smile and break a leg
Furniture
Is cracking up
The holidays are near

Contest of Opinions

Tito, toleration
Died
Slobodan thrived
Striped Kosovo of
Her autonomy, repressed
Albanian minority

July sunshine on
Independent Slovenia
But what of Tudjman?
What of Croatia and
Shelled Dubrovnik?

Contest of opinions
Sins?
Unity or slavery?
Ethnic cleansing
Dream or nightmare?
Republic of Serbian Krajina

Croatian defiance
Endurance no more
Shell and bullet holes
Scars of the
Serb population.

Mr Fox

No. Not what you said Mr Fox
Nor the upset caused
It was what you did not say
That most disturbed

With a broken philosophy
You built your den
To lie alone on pallid evenings
Your desert of sand and solitude

Deliquescent fox
Diffident to communicate
The wasted woolshed
Is soon forgotten

Wolf Moon

I took you from the wolves
Freed you from your past
Danced on a journey of
Majesty and mystery
Under the comforting constant
Illuminating the night sky

By the legend of the wolf rising
You captained your own ship
By the flowing tide
Moved on to Yonkers
The soft brush of silent snow
Embracing blizzard Jonas

The pink moon of April
Moved your mind
By May's abundant blooms and
The flower moon
You mastered
Your own fate.

18th Century Courtesan

Stolen pleasures with
Mr Dardis, Peg
Met the seduction halfway
Indulgence in
Georgian Dublin

Lover to Lawless
And Jackson
Kept by Mr Leeson
Happy endings on
Ranelagh Road

Pinking Dandies
Trinity thugs killed
Your unborn child
Traumatised, you took life
From your second

Assertive, strong you
Roared to the fore
Demanded
Robert Crosbie be
Hanged

Difficult to
Disrespect, you
Paid your dues
Pity Peg Plunkett was
Called an impure

Absolute

Was love the reason you departed?
Love the reason you left Darndale?
Compassion why you left behind
All that was good, sweet and beginning?
Compassion why your heart's blending?
Passion the reason your music lives?
Passion to guide us
To absolute freedom.

Dignity the reason joy's not around?
Dignity the reason you were Tennessee bound?
Was respect the reason you never returned?
Respect for the silence?
Was despair the reason for your buried grief?
Despair the reason you play your music
Somewhere we can no longer hear you?
Despair the reason for your burial ground?

Forensic Journey

Key to freedom
Beacon of hope for
The wrongfully convicted
World of shadows in a
Criminal justice system

Languishing in jail
Prosecuted on eye witness
Identification alone
For crimes not committed
Wheels of justice broken

Attorneys assessing evidence
Before its destruction
Mounting appeals
Mitochondrial DNA testing
Fearsome fighters

Crime scene DNA
Not matching the suspect
Hundreds exonerated
Georgia, Tennessee, Alabama
Escaping capital punishment

Indictment dismissed on
The DA's motion
Solving decades' old
Homicides
Conclusive proof of innocence

A woman found shot in
A field in California
Her murder unsolved
For thirty two years
Almost forgotten

Cold case squad
Submitted stored evidence
To the FBI lab
For DNA testing
Hair, saliva, skin, blood

Trepidation, excitement
Philip Arthur Thompson's
Profile matched
Already serving a sentence
In California state prison

Extraordinary cases
Constitutional rights
Unshakable
Moral conscience
An absolute

Eddie Albert Crawford
Twenty years on death row
Executed
With biological evidence
Still to be tested

Michael Graham
Fourteen years on death row
Prosecution withheld
Evidence of his innocence
Inexperienced Attorneys

Jimmy Ray Bromgard
Fifteen years in a
Montana prison
Before being cleared
By DNA testing

Post-conviction
Exonerations
Nothing less than
A devastating breakdown in
The meaning of Justice

Granny's Bonnet

Dusky pink eyes
Uninvited
Quietly unfolding
Approaching with caution
The day

Unannounced it is
Early June
A colourful sensation of offspring
Popping up in un-kept borders
Sprinkled amongst lettuce and cabbages

With past behind you
Softening the contours
Dancing with the sun
Removing your green dress
Letting nature do the gardening

Horribly invasive
Some will cut you
Display you
Smell you
Starve you

Beguilingly beautiful
Others will admire you
Desire you
Think of you in
Sonnets and poetry

How did you arrive in
My white stone garden?
Self -seeded progeny of
Parent plants, bought
Grown many moons ago

Given to me as a gift or
Sneakily distributed by the
Plants' woman in
Elphin before me
Sprinkle here, sprinkle there

Tiny seed hitching a lift
Stuck on the sole of a
Muddy boot
Concealed within the
Droppings of a passing bird

Granny's bonnet
Fun party crasher in
Our garden
Bubbles in my
Glass of champagne

Murmuration over Kinard

Senan
Building bridges
Barefoot in the
Ailfinn stones
As they transcend
Flocking starlings
Nature's most
Incredible sight

Holding hands
Hugging tight
Captured in the
Moment as
Thousands formed
Dark moving clouds in
The dusk sky over
Our house

Four minutes perhaps
Of wonder
Mesmerising and
So much more
Back to
Building bridges
Holding hands
Hugging tight

Substance

My butterfly's in love
With your butterfly but
Love must know its place
And the heart must
Go without

Let's take a walk
In silence where
The oceans are blue
Escape the tyranny of
Language for a while

Dream the dream
That is gently in us
Gaze patiently
Marvel at the waves
The pouring rain

Slowly awakening
Taking us back
To somewhere
Terrifying
Reality

Pointless said reason
Substance divine
In essence my soul lies
Parting from you now
On a wet tormented shore

The tears from those
Twinkling eyes trickling
Down the golden sand
The breaking of
Two hearts